DAVE & VIOLET

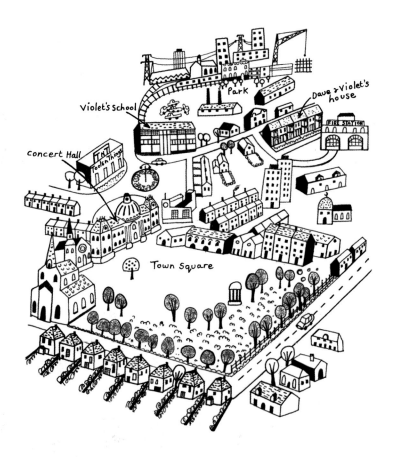

For Grace

Text and illustrations copyright © Sarah Adams 2011
The right of Sarah Adams to be identified as the author and illustrator of this work has been
asserted by her in accordance with the Copyright, Designs and Patents Act, 1988 (United Kingdom).

First published in Great Britain and the USA in 2011 by
Frances Lincoln Children's Books, 4 Torriano Mews,
Torriano Avenue, London NW5 2RZ
www.franceslincoln.com

A catalogue record for this book is available from the British Library.

ISBN 978-1-84780-052-7

The illustrations in this book are lino prints

Set in Humana Sans ITC

Printed in Heshan, Guangdong, China by Leo Paper Products Ltd. in October 2010

135798642

DAVE & VIOLET

SARAH ADAMS

F

FRANCES LINCOLN
CHILDREN'S BOOKS

When Dave the dragon was happy, his scales were all the colours of the rainbow, but when he was sad he was blue.

His best friend Violet thought he was very beautiful. However, not even Violet realised that Dave was very, VERY shy.

"Come to the park and meet my friends," said Violet one day.

Dave looked frightened.

"Please, they all want to meet you," she said.

Everyone crowded around Dave.

They had never seen a dragon before. Dave grew hotter and redder . . .

and hotter  and REDDER...

Then  SUDDENLY . . .

whoosh

Flames of fire gushed from his mouth!

Dave tried to say sorry,
but everyone ran away.

"Never mind," said Violet. "My school band is giving a concert. Why don't you come and play with us?"

Dave desperately wanted to be accepted,
so he practised very hard.

As the audience hushed to listen,
Dave grew hotter and redder and
REDDER, then suddenly . . .

whoosh

Flames of fire gushed from his trumpet!

No-one was quite sure what to make of his performance.
Dave tried to say sorry, but everyone ran away.
"Never mind," said Violet. "Perhaps you could get
used to people if you had a job. They're looking for
a dinner lady at my school."

Eager to please, Dave agreed, but secretly felt
very nervous. Seeing the long queue all staring at him,
Dave grew hotter and REDDER, then SUDDENLY . . .

whoosh

Flames of fire gushed from his mouth!

Everyone's lunch was burnt to a crisp!

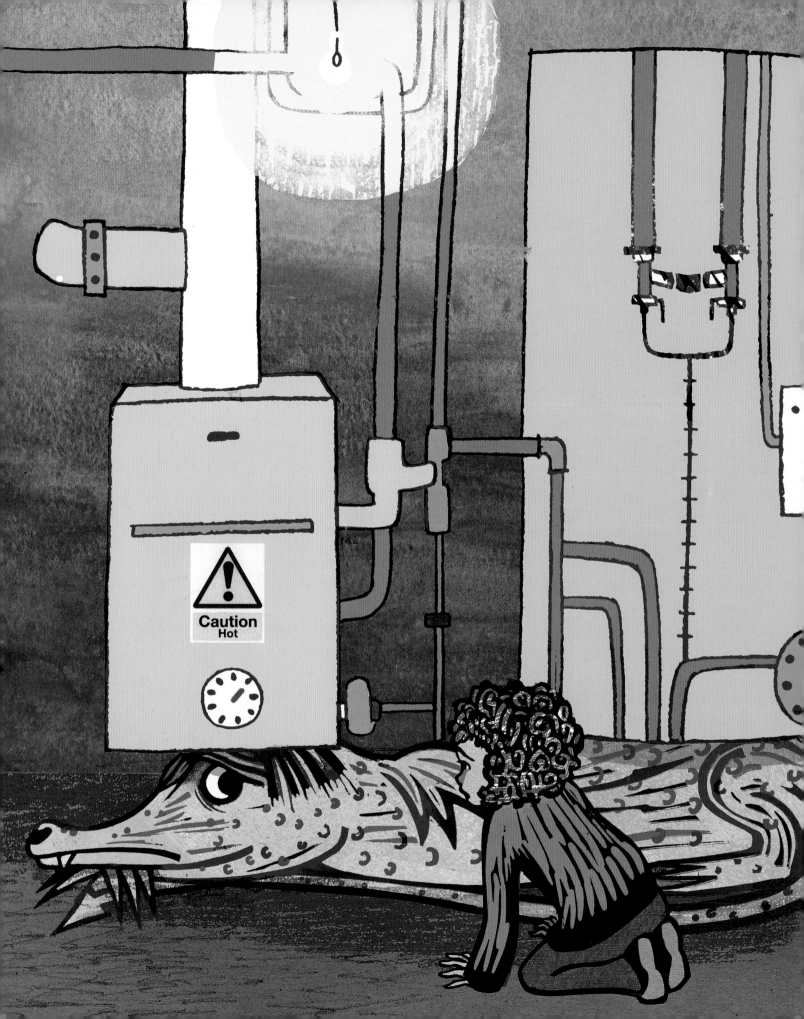

For days Dave wouldn't leave
the house. He hid in the cellar
feeling very sad.

"What use am I?" he said.
"The harder I try, the more
they hate me."

"Come on," said Violet
gently, "let's go out."

It was dark and raining as they walked down the road.
Dave felt very gloomy.

In the town square a large crowd of people were standing in a circle. They all looked gloomy too. Everyone stared. Dave grew hotter and REDDER, then SUDDENLY . . .

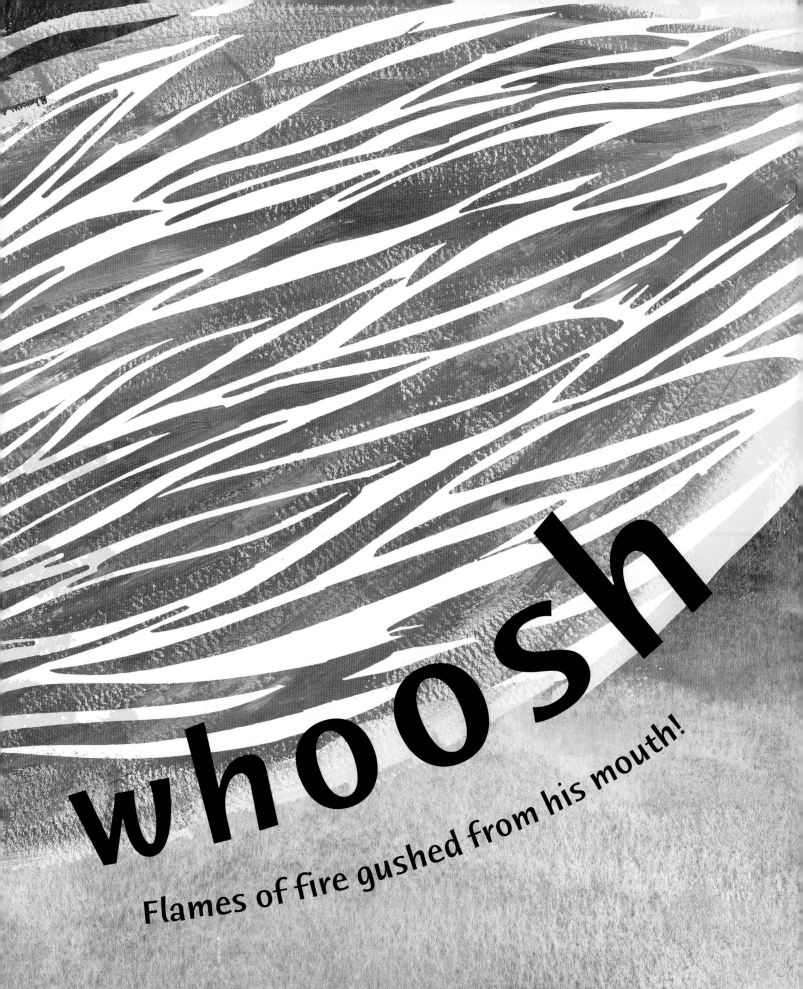

whoosh

Flames of fire gushed from his mouth!

But instead of running away, everyone gasped in wonder, clapping and smiling. The night sky had become a dancing blaze of colour.

"Well done Dave," congratulated the Mayor.
"Because of the rain, the fireworks wouldn't light.
Thanks to you the party can now begin."
"Three cheers for Dave!" everyone shouted.
Dave glowed with happiness as they all leaped around him.

"You see," said Violet, "I knew everyone would like you."